THREE COOL KIDS

Rebecca Emberley

Little, Brown and Company
Boston   New York   Toronto   London

First Edition

Library of Congress Cataloging-in-Publication Data

Emberley, Rebecca.
    Three cool kids / Rebecca Emberley. — 1st ed.
      p. cm.
    Summary: This retelling of "The Three Billy Goats Gruff" is set
in the heart of a city where an enormous rat tries to keep three
goats from crossing the street.
    ISBN 0-316-23666-7
    [1. Fairy tales. 2. Folklore.] I. Title.
PZ8.E523Th 1995
[398.2] — dc20   93-40113

                    10 9 8 7 6 5 4 3

                          WOR

Published simultaneously in Canada by Little, Brown & Company (Canada) Limited

                    Printed in the U.S.A.

Other books by Rebecca Emberley:

My Day • Mi Día
Let's Go • Vamos
My House • Mi Casa
Taking a Walk • Caminando
City Sounds
Jungle Sounds
Drawing with Numbers and Letters
Rebecca Emberley's Cut-Ups: A Book to Cut and Glue

Once upon a time, in a big, big city, in a small open lot, lived the Three Cool Kids: Big, Middle, and Little.

DELIVERIES

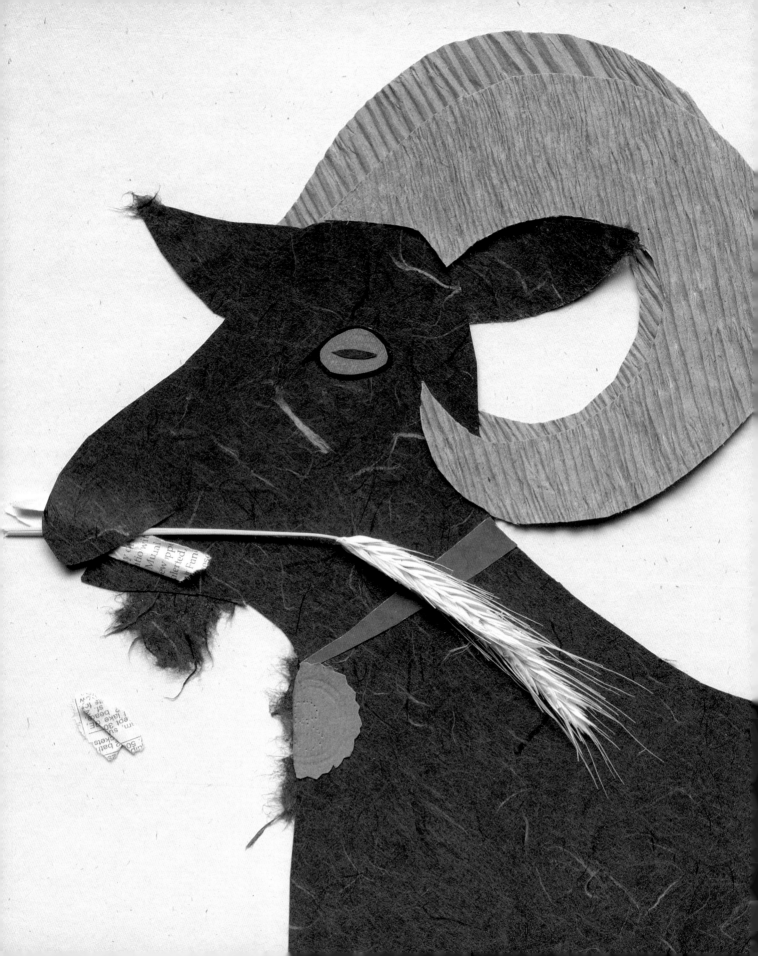

Big was the oldest of the three. He was large and dark, with great curling horns, of which he was very proud. Being both bossy and saucy by nature, he put himself in charge. He worked hard taking care of his brother and sister.

Middle was in between her two brothers, which is how she got her name. She was just a bit vain and wore many jingling silver bracelets. She was very proud of her brilliant white wool and spent most of the money she made from kid-sitting on lotions and potions for her gleaming curls.

Little was the youngest of the Three Cool Kids. He was very proud of his big brother and sister — and of his new red sneakers with purple laces. He was constantly prancing and dancing around, but he was careful when he played not to get his sneakers dirty.

The Three Cool Kids liked the lot that they lived on. They had been there for as long as any of them could remember. On two sides it had nice tall buildings that gave shade in summer and protected them from wind in winter. The front was open to the sun and had a good view of the neighborhood.

But after many years of grazing, the grass and weeds were getting sparse, and a great deal of construction was going on next door. They were taking down the tall buildings. The work was very noisy, dusty, and dirty. Soon they would be unprotected. They needed a change. They knew where they wanted to go.

Across the street and down the block, there was a vacant lot. It was full of sweet green grass and delectable weeds to eat. On one side of the lot, there was a beauty shop. That would make Middle happy. On the other was a recycling center, where Big and Little could find some work and maybe some delicious snacks. Oh, it was very tempting!

VACANCY

*AVID
RECYC

But something held them back from moving. They had all heard tales about a huge rat that lived in the sewer under the street. Everyone in the neighborhood had talked about it for years. No one had actually seen him, but terrible stories were told about those who had tried to cross the street and had never come back.

"It's just a rat," said Big. "I can't believe one sniveling, smelly little rat could be that bad."

"Hmmm," mumbled Little. "I wonder if he swallows you whole, or . . ."

"Oh, no," Middle groaned. "I don't like the sound of this! I think we should wait." So they stayed on their lot, hoping that someday things would improve, but they never did.

One day, when they were down to their last weed, Big decided that the time had come to move on. "I don't believe in fairy tales," he snorted. "We will cross the street." Middle's and Little's stomachs were growling, so they were easily convinced.

The Three Cool Kids trotted off down the block. They reached the corner and looked across the street. They could see the vacant lot and smell the sweet green grass. They stood there with their noses twitching. Little was so excited, he could not stand still.

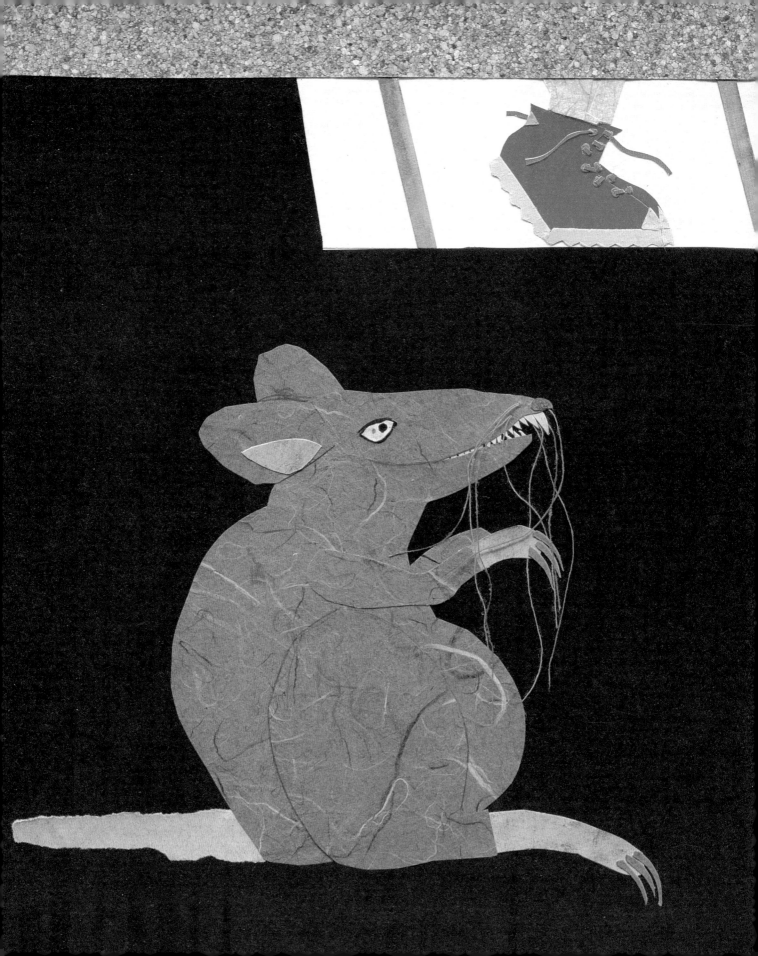

"I will go first," he offered, jumping off the curb. "I am not afraid," he muttered to himself. He started across the street. *Squincha, squincha, squincha*, went his sneakers. Suddenly, he stopped. He heard a terrible sound . . . and smelled a terrible smell. . . .

"Who is making that horrible noise on my street?" screeched a gruesome voice. Something peered out of the sewer grate with nasty yellow eyes. Little stood, trembling in his sneakers. He looked into the murky dankness of the sewer. It was a rat! The biggest, ugliest rat he had ever seen!

"It is only me, Little Cool," he said.

Sniff, snuff, went the rat. "You smell delicious! I think I will have you for my lunch!" And he poked his greasy whiskers through the grate.

"Oh! How rude!" bleated Little. "I am not for your lunch! My big sister is coming, and she will tell you what's what!"

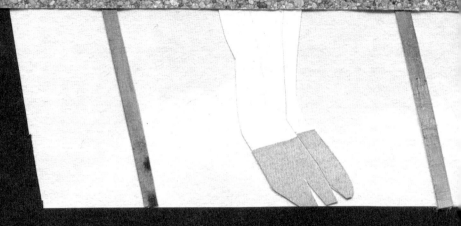

Kachinga, chinga, chinga. Middle's bracelets made a nice sound when she walked. Little felt better. He leapt onto the sidewalk. *Squonch!*

"Aiyeeeeeeeee!" shrieked the rat. "Who is making that frightful noise on my street?" Middle stopped. She smelled the rat's foul breath and shivered. "I-I-I am Middle Cool," she stammered.

Sniff, snuff, went the rat. "You smell sweet. I think I will have *you* for my lunch instead!"

"Oh! How rude!" shouted Middle. "I am not for your lunch! My big brother is coming, and he will tell you what's what!" She gave his slimy snout a wide berth and scrambled up on the curb. *Kachinga, chinga, chinga!*

All this noise had given the rat a headache. "I am really hungry now," he grumbled. "I wish I had something really big for lunch."

He was about to get his wish.

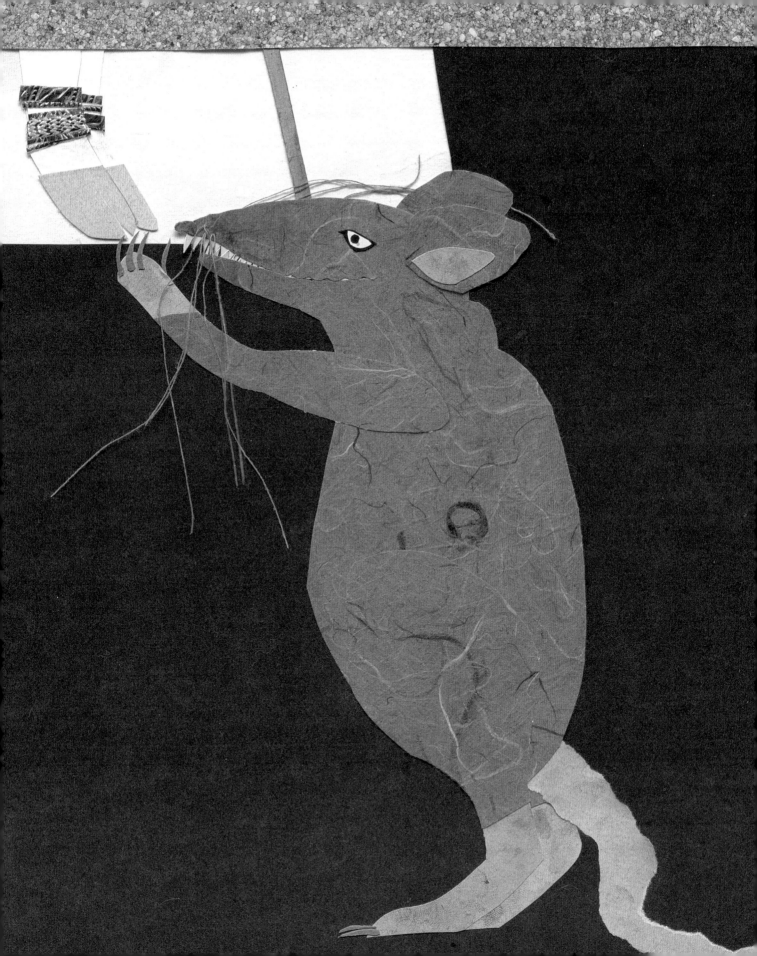

Big approached the sewer grate. *Kalomp, kalomp, kalomp.* "Yaaaaaaaaargh!" groaned the rat. "Who is making that monstrous noise on my street?"

"It's me, Big Cool," Big snorted. "What is your problem?" *Sniff, snuff.* "No problem now," growled the rat, licking his crusty lips. "You look big enough for lunch *and* dinner!"

But Big was not afraid. "You are a rude and repulsive creature!" he boomed. "No one has Cool Kids for lunch!" He stepped back and charged the grate. *Karangalangalangalang!* His great horns crashed across the bars.

"Yaieeeeeek!" wailed the rat, covering his ears, "I *hate* that noise!"

Big tromped on those filthy mottled whiskers and stared into those nasty yellow eyes. "Are you going to let me cross?" he asked.

"But I'm hungry," whined the rat.

"Listen, and I will tell you what's what!" Big thundered. "You will have to go elsewhere for your meals, and that is that!" He rose up on his legs and came down hard.

Karashalangalangabang! went his great horns on the grate. *Karonch!* went his hooves on the street.

Splash! went the rat as he fell back into the sewer. "I guess I'm not so hungry anymore," he sniveled as he floated away with the rest of the debris. He was never heard from again.

Big, Middle, and Little danced a little dance. *Squincha, squincha, squincha, kachinga, chinga, chinga, kalomp, kalomp, kalomp!* And they moved onto the new lot right then and there.

And if you ask them, they can tell you that the grass was very sweet on the other side of the street.